PREACHER CREATURE STRIKES ON SUNDAY

written by Mike Thaler
illustrated by Jared Lee

ZONDERkidz

ZONDERVAN.com/
AUTHORTRACKER
follow your favorite authors

To Bruce, for genesis.
—M.T.

To Mom, who always reminded her
young son that his talent was a gift
from God.
—J.L.

ZONDERkidz™

Preacher Creature Strikes on Sunday
Copyright © 2009 by Mike Thaler
Illustrations © 2009 by Jared Lee Studio, Inc.

Requests for information should be addressed to:
Zonderkidz, Grand Rapids, Michigan 49530

Library of Congress Cataloging-in-Publication Data

Thaler, Mike, 1936-
The preacher creature strikes on Sunday / by Mike Thaler ; illustrated by Jared Lee.
   p. cm. -- (Tales from the back pew)
ISBN 978-0-310-71589-4 (softcover) [1. Church--Fiction. 2. Christian life--Fiction.] I. Lee,
Jared D., ill. II. Title.
  PZ7.T3Pq 2009

[E]--dc22   2008007600

Editor: Bruce Nuffer
Art Director: Merit Alderink

Printed in China

09 10 11 12 / LPC / 5 4 3 2

Mom is taking me to church this Sunday. I've heard all about church.

You have to stand up, sit down, and kneel a hundred times.
It's a real workout. It's called being in the service—
I'm too young to get drafted!

And when you finally do get to sit down,
it's on hard wooden benches called *pews*. Pew!

Then you have to stay awake while some guy called a preacher tries to keep you up. And you have to be quiet.

God must like nuts,
because the only thing you get to say is *"Almonds."*

You do get to sing. There are very long songs with a thousand verses, and just when you think you're done, they go back to the beginning and start all over again. And you have to *stand* the whole time. It's sort of like the Pledge of Allegiance ... only longer.

And then, instead of paying you for singing, they collect money.

Next, the preacher gives a boring talk called a sermon.
At least you get to sit down.
But it can last for hours ... for days ... sometimes even for weeks.

That's why the preacher is called "The Sermonator."
I heard you might come to church and find people
from last week sleeping in the pews.

All the sermons are from the Bible.
It's a very thick book that God wrote.
I wonder if He used a computer.

It's full of stories about weird people.

One guy wandered in the desert for forty years.
He should have stopped at a gas station and asked for directions.

Another guy went on a forty-day cruise with a bunch of animals.
It rained every day! Too bad they weren't party animals.

A third guy also went on a cruise ... inside a fish!

Mom says God is invisible, and you can't see Him but He can see you.

← CHOCOLATE CHIP

She says He knows everything you do, good and bad. But God loves you no matter what, and someday wants you with Him in heaven.

Mom says heaven is more fun than an amusement park.
You get to be with God full-time and go on all the rides ... FREE!

 Well, here we are. It's Sunday, and we walk into church. Everybody's awake!

Everyone is friendly and says hello. I get to go off and play games, sing songs, make puppets, and act out Bible stories.

And I make lots of new friends.

We put on a play about a kid named David who beats up a big bully named Goliath.

The preacher says he was able to do that because God helped him. He says God will help us too, if we ask Him.

Then we have cookies and milk.

← PUPPET

PUPPY →

I love church. I wish every day was Sunday.
Mom says when you love God ... every day *is* Sunday!

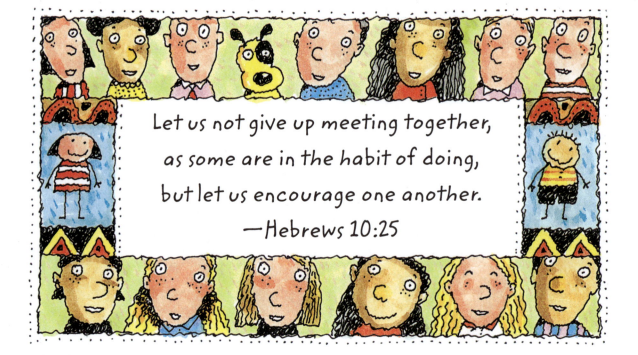

Let us not give up meeting together, as some are in the habit of doing, but let us encourage one another.

—Hebrews 10:25